Lizzie Dripping and the Witch

Lizzie Dripping and the Witch

Helen Cresswell

illustrated by
Chris Riddell

For my goddaughter Rachel,
who once lived in Lizzie Dripping's cottage

Published by BBC Children's Books
A division of BBC Enterprises Limited
Woodlands, 80 Wood Lane, London W12 0TT

First published 1991
This edition first published 1994

ISBN 0 563 40383 7

Cover printed by Clays Ltd, St Ives plc
Printed and bound in Great Britain by Clays Ltd, St Ives plc

Contents

Lizzie Dripping in the Rain

Once upon a time – and I mean last week, or last year – there was a girl called Lizzie Dripping. Her real name was Penelope Arbuckle, but nobody ever called her that. There is a girl called Lizzie Dripping in most villages round these parts. It isn't meant unkindly, it's really quite affectionate. It fits the kind of girl who is dreamy and daring at the same time, and who turns things upside down and inside out wherever she goes and whatever she does.

This is how *our* Lizzie Dripping was. She walked about with her head in the clouds, and was always trying to make life more exciting, more full of shivers and panics and laughter than it is if you leave it to itself. It often looked as if she was telling what people call fibs, but she wasn't, of course. She was just making things up as she went along, and that is quite a different thing.

I could tell you that Lizzie's father, Albert, was a plumber. I could tell you that her mother, Patty, had her feet as firmly planted on the ground as Lizzie had her head stuck in the clouds, so that it was a wonder the pair of them ever met. And then, of course, there was her little brother, Toby.

But the thing about Lizzie Dripping that you really need to know is that she had her own private witch. She had run across her one day in the graveyard. That witch had been sitting, cool as a cucumber, on the flat tombstone of *Hannah Post of this parish and Albert Cyril, beloved husband of the above 1802–1879 Peace, Perfect Peace.* What was more, she was knitting.

"Knit one, slip one . . . knit one . . . pass the slip stitch over!"

What she had been knitting was something black and lacy, for a witch baby. She had told Lizzie as much.

"I'm fed up with knitting. Fiddling, baby clothes is. Fiddle fiddle fiddle!"

She had a voluminous pocket somewhere deep in the black folds of her cloak, and into this she would thrust the knitting, pins and all, when she got cross. This was all too often.

What Lizzie's witch really liked doing was spelling. Lizzie had hardly known her five minutes before she had turned the Briggs's cat into a toad. (She had turned it back again more or less straight away, but that was beside the point.)

So Lizzie Dripping had to pick her way through life very carefully, between Patty, who was in charge of her life at home – visibly – and the witch, who seemed to be in charge of the rest of the world – invisibly.

The moment Lizzie stepped out of her house there was always the shiver, the exciting knowledge that that witch was about. Usually she was in the graveyard, true. But Lizzie had also seen her in the wide cornfields, in the greenish depths of the Larkins' pond and even, once, at the seaside.

One thing puzzled Lizzie a lot. Where was that witch

the *rest* of the time, when she was invisible?

"I'll find out one day," she promised herself.

That day came one wet Saturday in April. Lizzie had woken to hear the steady drumming of the rain on her window. She liked that. She lay listening to it, blowing in gusts, and could imagine herself at sea. Eyes shut and warm covers pulled under her chin, she half thought she could feel the bed rocking on a deep tide.

Then she remembered the picnic.

"Oh no!" She sat bolt upright, a landlubber again.

"Rain before seven, fine before eleven!" She looked at her clock. Half past eight. *Had* it been fine before seven?

She knelt on the bed and pulled back the curtains. The world was wishy-washy through the watery glass. Beyond the hedge and over the road the church tower was only a blur, and the sheep in the Home Field huddled under the half-leaved trees.

"Enough blue sky to make a sailor a pair of trousers?" She scanned the sky hopefully. There was not enough blue sky to make a sailor a vest, let alone a pair of trousers. There was no blue sky at all. "Unless there is at the back!"

Lizzie ran into Toby's room and peered out. Dripping bushes, wet roofs, a grey sky.

"Lizzie tum, Lizzie tum!" crooned Toby – which being translated meant, "Lizzie's come, Lizzie's come!"

Lizzie turned and looked at him crossly, snug and beaming in his barred cot.

"'S'all right for you!" she said. "You weren't going on a picnic."

She ran downstairs.

"Mam! Mam!"

Patty was busy, as usual, in the little scullery. Lizzie often wondered what she found to do in there all day.

"You up, are you?" was all she said.

"Was it rain before seven?"

"Was it what?"

"Rain before seven – you know, so as it'll be fine by eleven."

"I don't know, I'm sure," said Patty. "But it'll be raining all day, I shouldn't wonder. 'T'is April, Lizzie."

"Yes, but the picnic!"

"Well, that is a pity," agreed Patty. "Perhaps you could go next week?"

Miss Platt, Lizzie's teacher, was taking five of them on a picnic to Rufford Woods and Lake. It was to be a bird-watching picnic. There were hides, where you could watch unseen while the ducks and geese and moorhens went carelessly about their private, everyday business. There were woodpeckers and chaffinches and even tree creepers, Miss Platt said.

Just then there was a rattle of the latch, and next minute, "Oh – just look at my tights, all splashed and muddy they are!"

Aunt Blodwen was there. This was all Lizzie needed.

"Serve her right," she thought. "Why don't she wear trousers like anyone else?"

Aunt Blodwen was neat and dressy and always wore high heels. The very thought of her in trousers was enough to make Lizzie giggle.

Aunt Blodwen, who was now furiously shaking her umbrella, gave her a sharp Welsh look.

"And my perm – only just had it done. All of a frizz it'll be!" She hurried to the mirror to check. There was little to see of her hair, frizzed or not, under the neat grey hat.

"Came to see if the blouse had come, Patty," she said. "Out of the catalogue."

Lizzie groaned. Patty and Aunt Blodwen were always ordering things from the catalogue. Now, the next half hour would be spent trying on, twisting this way and that in front of the mirror, discussing colours and buttons.

"Going back up," she said.

She did not expect either of them to notice, and they didn't. She shook cornflakes into a bowl, added milk and sugar, and went back up to her room for a sulk. As she did so, she noted with satisfaction that Aunt Blodwen's umbrella was making a large puddle on the tiles. "Not that I expect Mam'll make *her* mop it up," she thought. "If it was me, she would."

She sat on her bed crunching the cornflakes and gazing out at the sky, in case a blue patch suddenly appeared. Because she could see the church tower too, she thought of the graveyard – and the witch.

"That witch," she thought, "wonder if she's out there now, this very minute? Sopping wet she'll be by now, if she is. And her knitting. But if she's *invisibly* there – would she be wet?"

This was the question that had been puzzling Lizzie for ages. And now, she suddenly realised, was the very time to find out.

"If I go to the churchyard and she's not there, I could call her. And then, when she appears, I'll see if she's wet or not!"

The idea was irresistible. She would then know for certain whether the witch lived in Lizzie's own world. Or whether, when she was invisible, she inhabited another, unseen world – one with its own sky and weather.

"And if so," thought Lizzie, "perhaps *I* could go there, one day. Oooh, smashing that'd be! There might be other witches there, hundreds of them. And p'raps I might even see that witch baby she's always knitting for!"

She had often tried, without success, to imagine a witch baby. You couldn't even *begin* to imagine a baby with a pointed chin and hooked nose.

The day, which had seemed spoilt, was beginning to look interesting, after all. Lizzie dressed, put on her wellingtons, and went down.

"The colour, more than anything . . . " Aunt Blod was

saying. "Got an olive skin, see."

Patty was sticking down a large flat packet.

"Oh, there you are, Lizzie. Take this up to the Post Office, will you? And make sure you get a certificate to show you've posted it."

The blouse evidently did not suit. Lizzie unhooked her anorak from the door.

"I'll wait here a bit, Patty," Aunt Blodwen said. "Just look at it! Drenched to the skin, I'd be. You take my umbrella, Lizzie. Might as well, as get another wet."

Lizzie grimaced. She took the umbrella, the parcel and the money and went out. The minute she was out there in the cool air with the rain slanting on her face, she felt better. She had no intention of using the umbrella. As a

matter of fact, she liked rain. She liked the sound and the smell and the taste and the feel of it. She stuck out her tongue and felt the tiny, cold stings.

"Drenched to the skin ..." she thought. "Wonder what it feels like? And the rain spattering you all over! Wish I could take all my clothes off and find out!"

And the thought occurred to her that she could do exactly that.

"No one about in the graveyard," she thought. "Specially today."

She trudged up the steep bank, through the wrought-iron gate and into the graveyard.

"Now, what first?" she wondered. "Drenched to the skin – or the witch?"

She decided that she could have both at the same time. She stepped inside the little west porch that was never used these days. There, she took off her anorak. She shivered.

"Catch my death," she thought. "Could."

She looked dubiously out over the long, beaded grasses and glistening tombstones. For the first time doubt crept in.

"Not right, really, undressing in a graveyard," she thought. "Don't suppose anyone ever has, not since the world began!"

Usually this was a thought that would appeal to her. Today, she was not so sure.

"Might show disrespect for the dead."

She decided on a compromise.

"Just my tee shirt," she thought, "and keep everything else on."

She peeled the shirt swiftly over her head.

"Brrrrrr!"

She stepped out of the porch. At once the skin of her arms and back and shoulders was being pecked by the sharp beaks of the rain. It felt marvellous, wonderful – better than sea spray, because the rain was driving and somehow alive. But it was cold, too, and so Lizzie tore down the path, right to the bottom, where a hedge divided the graveyard from the Larkins' pond. By the time she was there, she was well and truly sopping. She looked down and saw the water running down her front and arms, dripping from elbows and fingers. She was rinsed and shining with rain.

"Wheeee!" It felt just as good as Lizzie had imagined it would. "Why doesn't *everyone* do this when it rains? Wouldn't need umbrellas, then!"

She paused, tilting back her head and shutting her eyes. Then she ran back up the path, faster than ever, because a thought had struck her: "What if I get really hot and start *steaming*?"

When she had nearly reached the church, Lizzie stopped.

"The witch!" Was she there, behind the silvery curtain of rain? And if so, was she wet or dry? The stone slab where she usually sat was blank and shining.

"Witch?"

Silence. Silence except for the soft ticking of rain on stone and grass. If the witch were there, she was lying as low as the Perfectly Peaceful Posts.

"Witch! It's me, Lizzie!"

Silence. Then, hopefully, "And I'm drenched to the skin!"

She stood and waited, and all at once was cold, and shivered. She looked down and saw the goose flesh on her arms under the wetness.

"Brrrr! Get dressed, then find her!"

Round the side of the church she went and back to the porch, and, "Ooooeeh!" she gasped, and blinked with shock and the rain ran into her eyes.

There she was, her witch, a huddle of black rags in the far corner of the porch, as if tossed there, blown by the wind.

"Witch!"

The witch smiled, in a way Lizzie knew well, she smiled and waited. It was always the same. It was always Lizzie who had to speak first, find something to say.

"Look – I'm soaked!" Lizzie spread out her arms so that the water ran down and dripped off them. The witch looked, but without interest.

"Have you ever been soaked to – ?" She broke off sharply. "Oh, you've done it on purpose!"

The witch had chosen to come visible in the porch. She would be dry as a bone there, visible or invisible. Now Lizzie would have to wait for the answer to her question. And she suspected that the witch had *known* that Lizzie was trying to pin her down. She was grinning now, hugging her knees and rocking, her secret safe.

"Wet as a *toad*!" And she let out a high cackle.

Lizzie scented danger, as she always did when toads were mentioned. Having no wish to end up like the Briggs's cat, she stooped and picked up her tee shirt. It was difficult tugging it over wet flesh. And now she was cold, though whether from the wind or the powerful presence of the witch, she could not tell. She pushed her arms into her anorak and tugged it round her. All the time the witch watched.

"There. That's better!"

The witch blinked owlishly in her corner.

"*Was* going on a picnic today," said Lizzie, trying to get a conversation going – a safe conversation. "Can't now, of course. Bird-watching picnic. You go in a hide so's you're invisible, and – oh, *you* could, witch! You could watch birds – you're invisible nearly all the time!"

The witch could secretly watch thrush, blackbird, robin and finch, see them build their nests, twig by twig, and watch the patterns they made from dawn to dusk.

"What's that?"

Lizzie was startled. She followed the witch's gaze and saw Aunt Blod's umbrella, black and spiky. In the witch's world, rain or no rain, there were clearly no umbrellas.

"Brolly – look, I'll show you." Lizzie picked it up and opened it out, she was all at once under a low black cloud. "Keeps the rain off – see?"

The witch was on her feet now, skinny hands outstretched. She snatched the handle and skipped, cackling, out into the open, her long robes knocking rain drops off the grasses. "Eeee! Eeeheee!"

Off she danced, kicking her feet, umbrella twirled high aloft, above her pointed hat. She wove and skipped between the stones and bushes, still cackling, and threw out a fine spray, like a halo.

Lizzie watched laughing, because that fearsome witch had somehow changed, in a twinkling it seemed, into a child. She watched, and yet afterwards could not remember the moment when the witch was there, indistinct in a mist, and the next – gone. The cackling faded. Lizzie blinked.

"Witch! Oooo – Blod's brolly!"

Lizzie stumbled after her and knocked her knee, hard, against *Betsy Mabel Glossop aged 79*

Life's Work Well Done.

"Owch! Oh – witch! Come back, won't you!"

There was a sudden scatter and caw of rooks in the high trees, and Lizzie raised her eyes, half expecting to see the witch floating up there, umbrella and all, like Mary Poppins. The sky was blank and grey.

"Listen, witch!" Lizzie knew the witch could play hide-and-seek forever. "I'm going to Post Office, see, to post this parcel. You can play with . . . you can have the umbrella till then."

She marched back to the porch and picked up the parcel. She turned and addressed the empty, rain-soaked graveyard: "And when I get back, I want to find it where I left it! Are you listening?"

She expected – and got – no reply. Back through the iron gate she went and down the path by the memorial cross and there, with his bag of morning papers, she met Jake Staples.

"Where you been, Lizzie Dripping?"

"Never you mind."

"It's raining. It's pouring! What you been doing in this – ?"

She ignored him and broke into a run. She heard his voice blown after her.

"Up to summat, I know!"

"Hope he goes in there," she thought, "and the witch turns him toad. What he is, anyhow – a slimy toad!"

She posted the parcel and was leaving the Post Office when she met Miss Platt.

"Hello, Lizzie. Getting crisps and things for the picnic?"

"Picnic?" Lizzie echoed. "But it's raining!"

Miss Platt laughed. "It'll be dry enough in the hide. And real bird watchers don't let a drop of rain stop them."

"Oh, hurray!" Lizzie started back home to warn Patty. Sandwiches would be needed, after all. She was halfway home when she realised that the rain had stopped. She, too, stopped and scanned the sky for a patch of blue big enough to make a sailor's trousers.

"Funny, there isn't one. *That* ain't true, then. Not today, anyhow."

When she got home, Patty was feeding Toby in his highchair.

"That you, Lizzie? You've been long enough."

"Mam, Mam, we're going! I saw Miss Platt and she

says we're going! Shall I start buttering the bread?"

And she did butter the bread and spread the paste and make hot chocolate for her flask. Everything else went clean out of her mind. It was Patty, as usual, who brought her down to earth.

"Your Aunt Blod went, soon as the rain stopped. Said you could drop her brolly back to her. Better do it now, Lizzie, before you go. If she gets caught without her brolly, the heavens *will* open, and no mistake. Lizzie? *Lizzie!*"

But Lizzie was already speeding down the path and over the road and praying, "Let the witch be there! Let her give the brolly back! Let the – "

Bang! Smack into Jake Staples she went.

"Oooh, you – hey that's mine!" She snatched the umbrella from his grasp.

"Finders keepers – "

"No it's *not*!"

Despite her fury, Lizzie was thinking fast. She needed to know exactly where Jake had found the umbrella. If it had not been in the porch, but in among the stones and the long grasses . . . did the witch exist for Jake as well as for herself? "Where d'you find it, anyhow?"

"Ought to know, didn't you, if it's yours! Only you'd go leaving a brolly in graveyard, Lizzie Dripping!"

It was no use. Today was *not* the day when she'd find out if the witch came from another world with its own weather. And it was not the day when she would discover whether the witch was there, *really* there, for other people as well. She turned for home.

"Not my day," she thought. Then, up above the roof of her own house she saw bright blue sky – enough for a sailor's trousers and to spare. She started to run again. Perhaps it was her day, after all.

Lizzie Dripping and a Vanishing

The day started marvellously. The sun was shining, it was half term, and Gramma was coming to stay. Lizzie loved Gramma. She thought of her as a best friend.

"A best friend with wrinkles," she thought, and giggled. "Her *and* the witch, both wrinkled."

It was hard to think of the witch as a best friend exactly. For one thing, you never knew what she would spell next. For another, you couldn't invite her to your house, for tea.

Lizzie, who was picking flowers for Gramma's room, tried hard to imagine bringing the witch home for tea. She could – just – imagine her coming through the wicket gate and up the path, but as soon as she reached the door and knocked, Lizzie's mind simply went blank. The very thought of Patty and the witch face to face was unthinkable.

And then her sitting down to tea – next to Toby – and Mam saying, "Milk and sugar?" and making polite conversation, "Are you going anywhere nice for your holidays this year?" Imagine – that witch, on holiday! And then her pointy fingers snatching up the egg sandwiches. That witch – egg sandwiches?

There was no reason, really, why the witch shouldn't go on holiday – or eat egg and cress sandwiches.

"Wonder if she *does* go away from here, somewhere? And I wonder what she *does* eat?"

"Picking flowers, Lizzie Dripping? Does your mother know?"

It was Aunt Blod, clicking up the path on her sharp Welsh heels.

"She does, as a matter of fact," said Lizzie. "They're for Gram. She's coming today."

"Then I hope you'll be a help to your mam and keep from under her feet," said Aunt Blodwen. "Plenty of things a great girl like you can do to help."

"If I was a witch," thought Lizzie, "I'd turn you into a toad, and you'd stop that way!"

At the door Blodwen turned.

"Not forgotten Jonathan, I hope?"

As a matter of fact, Lizzie had. Jonathan was Aunt Blodwen's nephew, and had been to stay before. Lizzie quite liked him, and certainly felt sorry for him, having Blodwen as an aunt. (She wasn't Lizzie's real aunt at all – just Patty's best friend.)

"He'll be here by dinner time," said Aunt Blodwen. "And then you can go round the village, the pair of you, and give it a last tidy."

In she went.

"That's a nice way to spend your holiday," thought Lizzie, "picking up litter!"

Little Hemlock had been entered for the Best-Kept Village Competition. For months now people had been working overtime in their gardens, filling tubs and baskets and old sinks with flowers, and painting gates.

Aunt Blodwen, needless to say, was in charge.

"Shouldn't be surprised if she doesn't dust the flowers in her garden," thought Lizzie, "and hoover the grass and scrub the path. And when petals fall off, it's a wonder she don't sew them back on again, like buttons."

Her eye fell on Towser, slumped on the warm grass.

"You can't come litter picking, old chap," she told him. "It won't be a proper walk, for dogs."

She straightened up, and as she did so a cuckoo called away somewhere beyond the beeches. Her eyes went past the church and hedges to the fields and woods, shimmering in the early sun.

"Hope the judges'll see *them*," she thought. There was no doubt in her mind that Little Hemlock was the most beautiful village on earth, litter or no litter.

She went to put the flowers in water.

"Lucky I went in there," Aunt Blod was saying. "An absolute disgrace, and disrespectful to the dead."

Lizzie pricked up her ears.

"Spent no end of time on the chapel bank," Aunt Blod said. "Beautiful that is, neat as a pin. Anyhow, Mr Smith says he'll come over this afternoon and scythe it."

"Going to give the gravestones a good scrub as well, is he?" Patty enquired. "They're all over moss."

"You don't take things seriously, Patty," said Blod, "that's your trouble. And if Albert'll kindly pick up Jonathan at the station, that'll be lovely. Eleven twenty-two, mind."

And with that she was gone.

"Should be prime minister, that one," remarked Patty.

"What's she want to go meddling with the graveyard for?" demanded Lizzie. "It's smashing as it is. It'll look like any other graveyard with the grass cut."

"And you should know," Patty told her, "the time you spend up there. Look sharp with them flowers, Lizzie, I've a job for you."

Lizzie's mind was racing. If this Mr Smith went into the graveyard with his scythe, and started slashing and chopping – what about the witch? That witch was wild and flyaway, and Lizzie suspected that she liked her graveyard wild and flyaway, too. Lizzie couldn't somehow imagine her anywhere neat and tidy.

"P'raps she'll go," thought Lizzie. "Go right away, and never come back!"

The thought was unbearable.

"I'll have to warn her!"

And luckily, Patty sent her up to the shop for yeast and half a dozen eggs.

"And give Toby a push up," Patty told her. "Enough on today, without him bothering round me."

It was hard work pushing the chair up the steep bank by the church. Lizzie went through the little iron gate, then stopped. Now no one could see Toby from the road.

"Just stop here a minute, Toby," she told him. "Lizzie won't be long. Here!" and she pushed the apple she had snatched from the dresser into his sticky hands.

She hurried past the church and her eyes went straight to the stone where the witch would sit knitting – and there sat the witch, knitting!

"Ha!" she cackled, without looking up. "'S'you, is it! Knit one, slip one, knit two together . . . ."

"As if she'd *known* I was coming," thought Lizzie.

She advanced slowly. She left the path and waded knee-deep in the long grasses.

"Look, witch, I can't stop long," she began.

"Hmmm!" the witch snorted. "Nor can I, my girl, nor can I!"

"But I've just come to tell you . . . warn you . . . ."

The witch did look up then, her eyes green and narrow. Lizzie hesitated. Those were spelling eyes, toad-turning eyes. . . .

"The thing is ... Little Hemlock's in for the Best-Kept Village, and everything's to be tidied up by tomorrow. It's the judging, see."

"I ain't doing any tidying up!" snapped the witch. "So don't you think it!"

"Oh no – I didn't mean that! But the thing is ... they're going to tidy this." She waved her arms to take in the whole sprawling, overgrown graveyard.

"Don't need tidying," said the witch. "Everything in its proper place, ain't it? Grass in ground, birds in trees, dead in holes ... *toads* in holes . . . ."

"Just the grass," said poor Lizzie. "There's this man coming with a scythe to cut it."

There was a very long silence. The witch had dropped her knitting now and was looking about her, this way and that, surveying her kingdom.

"It ... it might look quite nice," ventured Lizzie at last.

"Nice? What's nice? Grass is green, grass is yellow, grass is *long*! *My* grass!"

And she vanished then – pouff – like smoke. Lizzie blinked.

"Witch – don't go!"

But the witch *had* gone – there was not so much as an invisible cackle. And Lizzie didn't have time to play hide-and-seek today.

"*I'm* going, then!" she shouted, and ran back up to the church, where Toby was stretching out his arms. His tiny fists curled and uncurled.

"Oh Toby – trust you!"

Lizzie picked up the apple from the ground, wiped it on her shirt, and gave it back to him.

Gramma arrived on the midday bus from Bilton, and Lizzie, as usual, went to the stop to meet her. She was wearing the black straw hat she always wore in summer. (In winter she wore a black felt one.) Lizzie hugged her.

"Near tall as you now, Gram," she told her.

"Little bones make old bones," said Gramma obscurely. "Well, my little duck, whole week off school, eh?"

And on they went to Briar Cottage, Lizzie carrying Gramma's bag and chattering on. She told about the Best-Kept Village, and how she and Jonathan would have to spend the afternoon picking up litter, but she did not mention the graveyard. Gramma was very fond of it, and often went in there. Today, the witch was in a dangerous mood, and Gramma was the last person in the world Lizzie wished to see turned toad.

As it happened, it was Patty who brought up the subject at dinner time.

"Blod's on the warpath," she informed Gramma. "Got the whole village tickled up so's you daren't hardly drop a pin, and now she's started on about graveyard."

"What's wrong with it?" demanded Gramma. "Looks no different from usual to me."

"Grass needs cutting, she says."

"It never in this world does!" said Gram. "Not meant to be parks, graveyards aren't."

"Got Mr Smith coming over this afternoon to scythe it."

"Smith?" echoed Gramma. "*Billy* Smith, you mean?"

“Him that never takes his cap off,” Patty said. “Sleeps in it, I shouldn’t wonder.”

“Billy Smith . . . ” Gramma looked pensive. “Sweet on me, he was, when we were young.”

They all stared at her.

"Always sending me little notes and bunches of flowers," she went on. "Used to hang round our house like a tom cat . . . ."

Still they stared, trying to see, beneath the grey curls and wrinkles, a young girl, one who drove the boys mad. Patty let out an incredulous laugh.

"Well, I must say!"

"Wanted to marry me, as a matter of fact," Gram said. "Might've done, I s'pose, if I hadn't met your father. There wasn't much to pick from, you know, in them days. Most folks ended up marrying school mates."

"I bet you were really pretty when you were young," said Lizzie loyally.

"Mind you," said Gramma, "I should've had to've been desperate. Idle? Bone idle. A born layabout. And from what I've heard since, never done a day's work in his life. Got ten children, though."

"And that's typical," said Patty. "His poor wife, that worked her fingers to the bone, I suppose."

"Dead," said Gramma. "Last year. I saw it in the paper. Still an' all . . . he had a way with him, Billy Smith . . . ."

And she smiled at her own memories.

"Aye, well, if he's as idle as you make out, he'll be hard put to get that graveyard mown," said Patty. "Less Blod stands over him, of course."

Lizzie winced. Billy Smith *and* Aunt Blod attacking the graveyard, and the witch, jealous of her long, waving grass, lurking.

"Anything could happen!" she thought. "Glad I'll be out the way."

Once dinner was over and washed up, Lizzie went to call for Jonathan.

"What'll you do?" she asked Gramma.

"Oh, a bit of this, a bit of that."

Lizzie nodded, picked up a dustbin bag, and went.

"A bit of this ... a bit of that ... just what I like doing," she thought. It seemed an eminently sensible way of passing a summer afternoon.

"One thing about getting old," she thought, "least no one can make you go round picking up other people's litter."

When she reached Aunt Blod's neat little cottage Jonathan was ready and waiting. They greeted one another awkwardly. It seemed ages since they'd last met, and in any case, Aunt Blodwen was there. That always made things stiff.

"*And* these, Jonathan!" she said. She was holding out a pair of pink rubber gloves, dangling like sausages.

"Oh, *must* I?"

"Of course you must! Where's your hygiene, boy? Picking up nasty dirty paper, and who knows where it's been. Where are yours, Lizzie?"

"Got none. Mam don't like rubber gloves. Says they make her feel funny."

"Whatever can she be thinking of? Sending her own child off round the gutters with her bare hands!"

She whisked open a drawer and whipped out another pair of rubber gloves – yellow, this time.

"Here we are. Now put them straight on, Lizzie, and don't take them off until you've finished. All those germs!" she shuddered.

"Biggest germ *I* know's *her*!" thought Lizzie. She pulled on the horrible, flabby gloves and knew instantly why Patty never wore them.

"Off you go now," Blodwen ordered. "Every little bit to be picked up, mind!"

The pair of them left, sheepish with their horrid pink and yellow hands. Neither said a word until they heard the door behind them shut. They turned into the road, behind the high privet, then stopped. They looked at one another properly now, as if this was their real meeting.

"Bossy bat!" Lizzie was already peeling off her gloves.

"Wish I'd never come," said Jonathan. "I'd forgotten what she was like. Must've."

Lizzie was puzzling what to do with the gloves. They couldn't go in the bag with the litter, and if she stuck them in the pockets of her jeans they still dangled out, waving as if they were alive. Jonathan, with a nervous glance behind him, peeled his off too.

"C'mon," said Lizzie. "We'll find somewhere to hide them."

Round the corner they went, and onto Back Lane. There was one house, and then the allotments, behind a high hawthorn hedge. Lizzie marched straight through the little wicket gate and Jonathan followed.

"Leave 'em here!" she announced. "Where no one'll see them."

She was about to stuff the gloves into the long grass by the hedge when her eye fell on a row of pea sticks. They were old Mr Green's. Here and there he had tied bits of paper, to keep the birds off. Lizzie giggled. She trod carefully down the row and dropped each glove over a stick.

"There! *They*'re bird scarers, all right! Scare the birds into fits, those will!"

Jonathan looked, grinned, and followed suit.

"We'll pick 'em up on the way back," Lizzie said.

After that, the afternoon didn't seem so bad. Every now and then they were so busy talking that they clean forgot they were picking litter, and had to retrace their steps.

"If she finds a single crisp packet she'll have my guts for garters," said Jonathan.

"Or even a sweet paper," agreed Lizzie. "Or a match-stick."

Into Church Lane they went, and then past Tenters Cottages. Down past the pub and the old mill, and then back to Main Street. People were in their gardens, putting the finishing touches. When they saw the pair with their bags they waved and smiled and told them how good they were. Old Mrs Stokes even gave them a bar of chocolate. They divided it, with their bare hands, and ate it.

Now they were nearly at the church. Up to now Lizzie had forgotten about Billy Smith and his scythe. Her eyes went fearfully up to the steep bank, half expecting to see the witch there, dancing with rage. She stopped and listened, but heard only the whistle of birds. You couldn't see the graveyard from the road. She simply had to know what was going on in there. But first, she had to get rid of Jonathan.

"Phew!" she said. "I'm boiled!"

She ferreted in her jeans pocket.

"Here – fifty pence. You nip up to the shop and get us a drink, and I'll wait here and watch the bags."

"Why can't you go?" he demanded.

"Because," said Lizzie sweetly, "it's my moncy. I'm paying."

He nodded, took the money and went. Lizzie watched for a moment, then towed the bags into the driveway to the church. Up the bank she scrambled, through the iron gate and down by the side of the church. There she halted.

The graveyard sloped away before her, hot and basking and as silent as ever she'd known it. The grass, honey coloured and heavily seeded, was knee-deep among the leaning stones.

"*Not* cut!"

Where, then, was old Billy Smith and his scythe? She looked at her watch. Nearly four.

"He must've come by now!"

The afternoon was nearly gone. Lizzie hardly dared think what she did now think. What if the old man had come, as promised? And what if the witch had been secretly there, watching? And what if, the moment he raised his scythe, the witch had snapped her fingers and –

Lizzie groaned. She knew it was possible. She had seen with her own eyes the Briggs's cat turned toad.

"Witch!" she screamed. "Witch!"

"Hello, there!"

Lizzie nearly jumped out of her skin. That voice was not the one she had expected. It was – she whirled about.

"You here again, our Lizzie?"

It was Albert. His eyes went over the graveyard, puzzled.

"Well, that's a rum 'un!" He shook his head.

"What? What're you doing here, Dad?"

"Come to tell the pair of 'em there's a cup of tea going. Your mother sent me to tell 'em."

"Tell – who?" quavered Lizzie. Mr Smith *and* Aunt Blodwen? Were there two brand new toads in there among the long grass?

"Your gramma and Billy Smith."

"Gramma?" Lizzie's voice came out as barely a whisper. Her lips felt stiff and numb.

"Where she *said* she was going." He seemed not to notice Lizzie's shock. "Go over to't graveyard and have a talk to Billy Smith, for old times' sake. That's what she said."

"And that's what she did," thought Lizzie. "Must've. And now she's toad, and could stop one forever. Oh Gram!"

She was close to tears.

"Bit of a mystery, that," said Albert. "Grass supposed to be cut, isn't it?"

Lizzie nodded. She could not speak.

"Well, best go and tell Patty."

He turned and lumbered off. Lizzie waited till he was out of sight and then, "Witch! Witch!" she whispered urgently. "Oh please, witch, *please*!"

Never before had she been so desperate for that witch. Never before had she felt so helpless, so powerless. That witch was not her puppet. She had a will of her own, did as she pleased.

"I'll do anything, if you'll just change 'em back! Honestly – anything!"

Then she heard a cackle, a high, mirthless cackle, splintering the warm silence.

"Witch!" Lizzie whirled this way and that, but could see not a sign of her. The witch was there, but invisibly there, as so often before.

"Hey – Lizzie!"

She groaned. Jonathan stood waving by the corner of the church. She went to join him.

"Quick, come on! Aunt Blod's coming!"

They scrambled back down the bank, picked up their sacks and hurried over to Church Lane, out of her sight. Lizzie opened her can and tilted it.

"Nearly done now, anyway," Jonathan said. "Any chance of me coming to your house for tea?"

Lizzie did not think so. She hardly dared picture the scene at teatime, with Gramma missing, presumed toad.

"Not that they'll ever know," she thought, "unless I tell 'em. They'll just think she disappeared."

"Not today," she told him. "Sorry. Gram's only just come, see."

On they went, trailing their bags. They stooped and picked, stooped and picked, and Lizzie felt unreal, as if she were in a dream – a nightmare. They had just reached the Post Office when Lizzie, straightening, saw Aunt Blodwen ahead. Lizzie would always avoid an encounter with her, but today she absolutely could not bear the prospect.

"Her fault!" she thought fiercely. "*Her* fault my gram's gone!"

She turned and ran, trailing her bag behind her.

"Lizzie!"

She heard Jonathan call after her, but did not care. On she pelted and round the corner into Church Lane again, just in time to see an old car drawing up outside her house. Out of one side climbed a grey-haired man with a cap, and out of the other – !

"Gramma!" Lizzie screamed, and ran towards her, and as she did so, the grazed bag finally burst. Lizzie dropped it. Much she cared.

"Oh, Gram, Gram, where've you been? I thought – "
She stopped dead.

"Fancied a little drive into Newark, to the market," said Gramma placidly. "Didn't I, Billy?"

Billy nodded and beamed and shuffled his feet, and for a fleeting moment Lizzie could *see* her Gram as the young girl who drove the boys wild.

"You'd best be off for your tea, Billy," Gramma said. "Best leave the grass. Half-cut graveyard's no use to anyone."

Lizzie Dripping, ankle-deep in litter, laughed out loud now. Her clever gramma was not turned toad. She had taken her old sweetheart off to market, and right out of the way of the graveyard and Aunt Blod. The witch's sea of grass was safe now.

As she went inside for a new bag she could smell new-made scones, and felt almost unbearably happy and light-headed.

Up on Mr Green's allotment, on the peasticks, waved four flabby-fingered gloves, frightening the pigeons and starlings into fits. Next day, they gave the judges of the Best-Kept Village quite a jump, too. Not to mention Aunt Blodwen. . . .

Lizzie Dripping by Moonlight

Lizzie Dripping often felt a prickle at the back of her neck when she read a poem she liked. It was rather like the prickle she felt whenever she went tiptoe and breath-held into the graveyard to see if the witch was there – *her* witch. Not exactly the same, because with a poem it was a prickle of delight. With the witch it was fright and delight.

Although Lizzie thought of her as *her* witch, and a friend of sorts, she was a tricky customer. She came and went as she pleased, refused to tell her name and was quite capable of turning cats into toads.

Slowly, silently, now the moon
Walks the night in her silver shoon;
This way, and that, she peers, and sees
Silver fruit upon silver trees.

Lizzie, who up till now had been daydreaming, as usual, felt that delicious, slow tingle along her spine. Her teacher was a good reader, and she picked good poems. Lizzie listened spellbound and the tingle was still there when the poem ended.

A harvest mouse goes scampering by,
With silver claws and silver eye;
And moveless fish in the water gleam,
By silver reeds in a silver stream.

Miss Platt's voice stopped. Lizzie waited. Surely there was more? She wanted the poem to go on and on.

"Is that all?" she asked. The rest of the class tittered and Lizzie felt her face fire.

"I'm afraid so," said Miss Platt. "Though you could always try writing another verse of your own." So she could, thought Lizzie Dripping. And she might, at that. But what she already longed for was to see a silver world of her own.

Was it *really* silver, at night, under the moon? Did trees, hedges, field and farm gleam and shine as if brushed with frost? Would the cows have silver eyes, and the sheep? Best of all, would she *herself* be silver?

At dinner time she asked Patty.

"Mam, does the world really go silver at night?"

"What?" Patty was dishing out the shepherd's pie, and only half listening, as usual. "Does the what?"

"World go silver. At night. When there's a moon, I mean."

"That's just your daft kind of question, Lizzie Dripping," her mother told her.

"Bit difficult to tell, these days," said Albert. "It's the street lights, see. Neither moon nor stars, when there's street lights. But in the old days ... aye ... I reckon it *was* kind of silvery."

"Then you've different eyes from *mine*," Patty told him. "Silver!"

And just then Toby set up yelling, and that was the

end of that. It was the end of the conversation, at any rate. But Lizzie Dripping went on thinking and what she wondered now was whether the moon was full.

That night, after Patty had gone back downstairs, Lizzie climbed out of bed and drew back the curtains. She could see the dark shape of the church tower and the sheep under the apple trees in the field opposite. The street lamps were orangey when you looked at them, but they didn't give a golden light. Lizzie's gaze travelled upwards and – her breath caught in her throat – the moon! It was there, full and round and white, hanging above the roof of Bell Brigg farm. Lizzie's spine dissolved into a long, slow tingle.

"Tomorrow," she thought. "Tomorrow night!" Because Lizzie Dripping had already decided that if there *were* a silver world out there, she was going to discover it. "I'd have to go out the village," she thought, as she lay plotting her plot. "In the fields, where there's no light." The thought was a little frightening, though she didn't see why.

"There'll only be sheep and cows," she thought, "and mice and that, with silver claws and silver eye." Then, "The witch!"

That was a very different kettle of fish. If Lizzie was to go walking out of Little Hemlock alone, at night, then the last thing she wanted to know was that the witch was about. A witch in broad daylight and only a stone's throw away from home was one thing. A witch at night, by moonlight, was definitely another. There was only one thing to do.

Next day was Saturday. Lizzie, as usual, was sent up to the shop, and as usual was told to give Toby a push.

"Does he *have* to go?"

Lizzie was going to call at the graveyard, as well as the shop. "I think he's bored with being pushed to the shop."

"Of course he ain't, are you, my lamb?" Patty lifted Toby and plonked him in his pushchair.

"You're a nuisance," Lizzie told him as she pushed him down the path. "Toby Arbuckle's a great fat nuisance, Toby Arbuckle's a great fat nuisance!" Toby gurgled plumply and waved his knitted cat by the tail.

"Well, don't blame *me* if you get turned toad!" Lizzie told him. A while back, she had seen with her own eyes the Briggs's black and white tom turned into a toad. Luckily, the witch had been in a good mood that day, and had turned him back again.

"If that witch turns *Toby* into a toad, I'll never be able to go back home again," thought Lizzie Dripping. "Not ever."

Up at the shop she bought the things for her mother and then spent part of her pocket money on sweets for Toby. "To keep him quiet," she thought. "Then I'll push him into the church porch, where the witch can't see him."

Though she could not be sure, not absolutely sure, that the witch *wouldn't* see him. For all she knew, that witch could see through stone. She reached the church and pushed Toby by the steep, grassy bank that she always thought of as a pathway into the sky. When she reached the little wrought-iron gate at the top she stopped and listened. Only the whistle of birds, the soft sough of wind in the seeding grasses, the bleat of lambs from the Home Field. Lizzie took a deep breath and went through the gate. She wheeled Toby into the porch, then gave him the sweets.

"You stop here, Toby," she told him. "Lizzie'll be back soon." As she turned the corner of the church her eyes went straight to the wide flat tomb of *Hannah Post of this parish and Albert Cyril, beloved husband of the above 1802–1879 Peace, Perfect Peace*. That was where the witch would sit, endlessly knitting in black wool what looked like a shawl for a witch baby. Not there!

Lizzie was not surprised. The witch could make herself visible or invisible in the blink of any eye. And she liked playing hide-and-seek. Lizzie called softly.

"Witch? Witch, where are you?" No reply. Not even the twitch of a grass by the tomb of the Perfectly Peaceful Posts. "It's me! Lizzie!" Silence. Then – Lizzie stiffened – a thin, high cackle from somewhere near, somewhere behind her. Round she whirled. Nothing. Not a sign.

"Knit one, purl one, slip one, knit one, pass the slip stitch over . . . ."

Slowly, breath held, Lizzie turned again. There she sat, her witch, hunched over her tattered knitting. "I spy with my little eye!" The witch did not even look up.

"Oh witch! You *are* there!" Lizzie edged closer, but not too close. "It looks smashing. Your knitting, I mean."

"'S'all right," said the witch. "What d'you want?"

"Oh! Oh, nothing," Lizzie lied. "Just wanted to see you, that's all."

The witch did look at her now, with her fierce bright eyes. It was as if she could see right through Lizzie – read her thoughts, even. Lizzie swallowed hard.

"Witch . . . ."

"Well? What is it, girl?"

"I wondered . . . I mean, when I come to see you, it's always daytime, see. What I wondered . . . is . . . do you come at night, as well?"

"Day, night, sun, moon – 's'all the same to me!" The witch's black mittened hands were working her needles again.

"So – you do come out at night?"

"Maybe do – maybe don't!" said the witch unhelpfully. Click click went the wooden needles. Lizzie decided to try another tack.

"Witch – there's a full moon. When there is . . . is . . . does the world turn silver?" The witch stuck her pins into the ball of wool and thrust her knitting deep into the black folds of her cloak. She sat then, musing, rocking a little from side to side. And when she did speak, it was in a dreamy, singsong way, as if to herself. "Moonlight

. . . owl light . . . bat light . . . " she crooned, "*witch* light . . . ."

"Oh dear," thought poor Lizzie Dripping. "She *does* come out at night."

"Bats fly, owls hoot, witches ride . . . and the moon's huge and white, and the whole world's . . . " she paused.

"Yes?" prompted Lizzie softly, hardly daring, "Yes?"

"Silver . . . ." The witch whispered the word, stroked it, as if it were a cat. "Silver!"

"Ah . . . " Lizzie let out a long held breath. So the witch did inhabit the world of the night and the witch saw a world of silver at every full moon. "Oh," she said, and now she too was speaking her thoughts aloud. "Oh, I'd give anything to see it, anything!"

"Then see it, girl, see it!" the witch snapped. She was back to her usual self again now, tart and crabby.

"But I can't! I mean . . . I mean . . . ."

"Daren't?" suggested the witch slyly, tilting her head. "Daren't – because of me?"

"Yes. No . . . oh, I don't know!" Lizzie was almost in tears now.

"But *I* know." The witch looked at her now, very long and hard. "*I* know . . ." And as she spoke, she vanished. She did not vanish in a twinkling, as she usually did. She faded, dissolved into the green air by the hedge. Lizzie strained into the shadows, but there was not the least hint that the witch might still be there, even invisibly there.

"Witch?" she called. "Witch?" She wheeled about, scanning the leaning, barnacled tombstones, the knee-high grass and wind-bent trees. The world was suddenly empty and bleak, as it always was after the witch vanished.

"But she's there somewhere," Lizzie comforted herself. "Must be. Invisibly there."

Then she remembered Toby, and found him smothered in chocolate in the church porch. He beamed, a sticky beam.

"Look at you! Just look at you!" The smile faded. The round blue eyes fixed anxiously on Lizzie's. In a flash she was contrite. She had spoilt his morning just as the witch had spoilt hers.

"Oh Toby! 'S'not your fault! Come on, sausage – Lizzie loves you!" And she swept him up from his chair, chocolate and all, and hugged him. And even as she did so, she knew that it was as much to comfort herself as him.

The rest of the day, the long stretch that lay between sun and moonlight, was long and unsatisfactory. Lizzie loved Saturdays, as a rule. She dawdled and dreamed her way through them as sleek and happy as a cat – if Patty let her. Today, she could settle to nothing. The world itself seemed drained of colour, drab and dull. Lizzie's thoughts were fixed on another world entirely – a silver one. She felt that she would die if she couldn't see it. To relieve her feelings she *did* write another verse to the poem Miss Platt had read:

I walk the night down the quiet lane
White and shining as if with rain,
Down to the fields where lie in peace
Silvery sheep with their silver fleece.

She was quite pleased with it, in a way. "Only thing is, it's a cheat," she thought. "I haven't been down the lane at night, nor seen silvery sheep." What was worse, she couldn't be sure that she ever would. For all she knew, she had that witch for life. And now she knew for a fact that the witch came out at night.

She would be there, lurking in the spiky shadows, brimming with spells. And Lizzie Dripping felt in her bones that night spells were dangerous, not to be sneezed at.

"Dare I?" she wondered. "Or daren't I?" She never gave a thought to Patty, and what she would say if she found that Lizzie was up and out by night, walking the fields alone in the moonlight.

"Easy enough to slip out," she thought. "They'll be watching the telly and never notice." Even if, by some stroke of ill luck, Patty did find out, it was not the end of the world. But if, out there in the wide, moon-bleached fields, she met a witch – that might be the end of the world.

It went on all day. "Dare I . . . daren't I? Dare I . . . daren't I?" In the end, she didn't have to decide. It was at teatime when the blow fell. "Lucky Blod was free,"

Lizzie heard her mother say, "else we couldn't've gone."

"Gone where?" demanded Lizzie.

"Whist Drive, tonight, at the village hall. Your Aunt Blodwen's coming to babysit."

"Oh no!" It was one thing to get past Patty and Albert, another thing entirely to get past Aunt Blod, with her sharp Welsh eyes and sharp Welsh ears. Lizzie's beautiful world of silver splintered like glass before her eyes. "Now I'll never see it," she thought. "Never. Not till

the next full moon, anyhow." But the next full moon was light years away, an eternity. "I'll die," thought Lizzie Dripping. "I'll just die." She told herself this quite often.

At just before seven Aunt Blod arrived with her knitting, and Albert and Patty went off.

"Bed at eight, mind, Lizzie," Patty called as she went.

"I'll see to it, Patty," Blod said. "Don't believe in

children up all hours, watching telly and ruining their eyes." The back door shut.

"I don't watch telly," Lizzie told her coldly. "I read."

"Ruin your eyes just as easy reading," said Aunt Blod smugly. "Eight o'clock, Lizzie, and not a moment after."

In the end, Lizzie went to bed early. Better to lie in bed reading than stop with Aunt Blod and the click click click of her needles.

"Nearly dark!" Lizzie peered through the curtains. The moon was already hanging there, but pale and washed out. The street lamps glowed orange and she could see the lights of the village hall by the church.

"If ever I'm prime minister," she told herself savagely, "there'll be a law against street lamps!" She dropped the curtain and climbed into bed. She had a good book – one about a boy who was snatched away by an eagle – but she could not keep her mind on it. All the time, mixed in with pictures of the soaring eagle, were other pictures of a world in the moonlight, a silver world.

After about an hour she gave a sigh and looked at the clock on her bedside table. Nearly nine o'clock. "Dark outside, now," she thought. "At least, dark except for the moonlight. Just finish this chapter and – oh!"

The light went out. At the very same moment the music and laughter from below, where Aunt Blod was watching television, stopped dead. For a moment there was darkness and silence. Then a shriek from Aunt Blodwen.

"Electricity cut," thought Lizzie. They had them, from time to time, and Patty always had candles ready. She could hear Aunt Blod stumbling about below, looking for them. Lizzie lay there, and as she did so became aware that the room was no longer dark. Her eyes went to the curtains – the pattern was showing, as it did first thing in the morning.

"The moon!" Lizzie was out of bed and at the window and then staring out at a new world. She had known the scene all her life, but now it lay foreign, strangely other under a broad, white light. The street lamp had been snuffed out like a candle and the moon had come into its own. Each apple tree in the orchard below was dappled silver and stood anchored in a sharp black shadow. The grass was bleached as if thick with hoar frost. Here and there lay the sheep. "Silvery sheep with their silver fleece! 'S'true then. The world *does* turn silver."

Down below Aunt Blodwen was muttering to herself, still searching for candles. Lizzie did not even hear her. She was gazing out at a world that till now she had hardly dreamed of, and thinking what a miracle it was that all the lights should go out tonight, of all nights. A miracle, or – the witch!

Was she out there, stalking the silver night, rubbing her skinny palms with glee? Could a witch make the lights go out?

Lizzie Dripping leaned right out of the open window and the moon shone full on her face and she could have sworn that she actually felt herself turn silver.

"Witch?" she called softly. "Witch! Thank you, witch."

An owl hooted mournfully from the beeches down below. There was a sudden screech – which might have been that of a moorhen by the lake, frightened by a fox. Or might have been that of a witch . . . a silver witch?

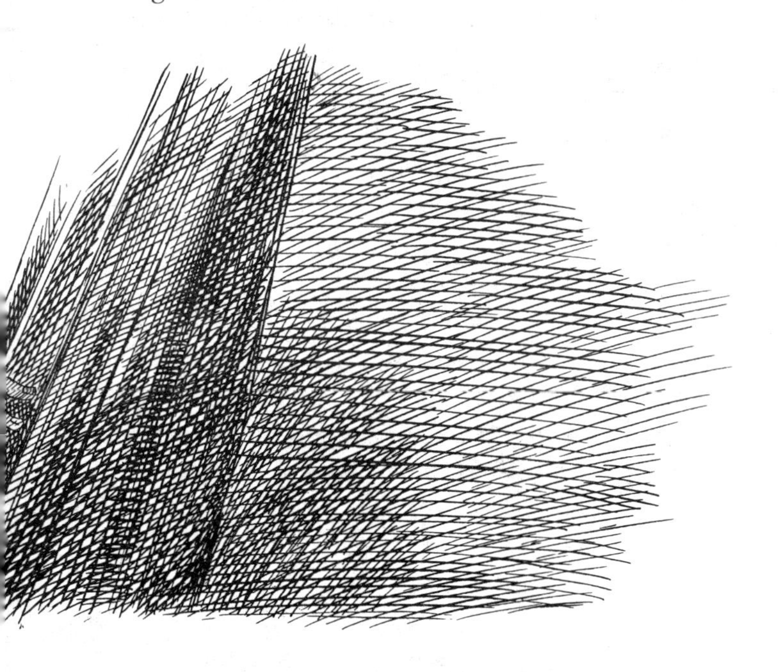

Lizzie Dripping goes to London

"It was your Dad's idea," said Patty. "Wasn't it, Albert?"

"Treat, I thought," he said, looking awkward. "Treat for you, Lizzie."

"Me, and all," said Patty. "Years since I've been to London."

"You get these cheap day trips of a Saturday, see," explained Albert, as if this, rather than his own kindness, was the real reason for going.

"Oh yippee!" cried Lizzie. "Tomorrow?"

"Your Aunt Blod'll have Toby," said Patty. "We can't be trailing him round shops all day."

"Not shops, Patty," said Albert. "Remember? Treat for Lizzie, this is."

Lizzie felt she might actually burst with pride and pleasure. They were going on the train all the way to London for *her*! And Toby wasn't even going! It often seemed to Lizzie that the whole household revolved round her little brother – certainly as far as Patty was concerned. He sat like a lord in his high chair and was waited on hand and foot, kissed and cuddled from morning till night. Whereas it was, "Lizzie do this, do that, fetch this, fetch that," not to mention, "Don't do this, don't do that!"

And as for treats! Lizzie had always thought these were for birthdays – big ones, at any rate. Patty did sometimes think of little treats.

"Fetch the chip pan, Lizzie," she would say out of the blue, halfway through an evening, "and you and me'll have a nice plate of egg and chips. I could just fancy it – could you?"

And Lizzie would nod, and the pair of them would sit and guzzle like conspirators, with Toby safely away in his cot and Albert out on a job. Those chips always tasted better than any others – chips fit for a king.

Lizzie was bursting to tell someone the news and decided on the witch.

"Might never even have heard of London," she thought, "let alone been there." Though, of course, she could not be sure. For all Lizzie knew, that witch might secretly wander the whole world, the universe, even.

Towser was lying outside the door and when Lizzie came out rose and stretched and wagged his tail hopefully.

"Not now, Towser, old chap," she told him. Then, lowering her voice, "Going to see that witch, see."

So far, Lizzie had not dared to take Towser with her on her visits to the graveyard. She had an uneasy feeling that the witch was not a dog lover. She had sometimes tried to imagine her walking a dog on a lead, but simply could not.

"If *she* had a pet, it'd more likely be a dragon," thought Lizzie. "Or a wolf."

Towser, who was an Old English Sheepdog, looked not at all like a wolf.

"Stay!" she ordered now, and he sank down again, raising brown, reproachful eyes.

As she rounded the corner of the church, Lizzie saw that, for once, the witch was already there. She halted. The witch was not knitting, or even reading, as she sometimes did. She was hunched in what looked like a terrible, black sulk. Lizzie, eager as she was to share her news, hesitated. If anyone could stop her going to London tomorrow, that witch could.

"Do anything, she can," thought Lizzie. "P'raps I'd better not . . . ."

"Well?" snapped that familiar, cracked voice. "Now what?"

Lizzie gulped. The witch had known she was there, without even looking up. She took a few steps forward.

"N-nothing, not really," she said. "Just came to tell you something."

Though now she wished she hadn't. Her eagerness to share her marvellous news had gone, evaporated the moment she saw that bunched, black bundle.

"What?"

Still the witch was not even looking at her. She was a tricky customer at the best of times, but today she seemed more than ever unknowable. She might do anything, it seemed. She was out of patience with her knitting, out of patience with her book, out of patience with the whole world.

"I shan't tell her, not now," Lizzie decided. "Might do something to stop me, out of spite."

"Well?"

"Oh dear, oh dear," thought poor Lizzie. "Now I shall have to tell a fib. What shall I tell her? Quick, Lizzie, think of something."

Still she stood, quaking, by the tomb of *Betsy Mabel Glossop aged 79 years Life's Work Well Done.* Lizzie Dripping was not very good at telling fibs. If ever she did, she always had a terrible feeling that the fib was haunting her, following her everywhere, and sooner or later would spring on her, and she'd be found out.

"It – it's nothing, really," she quavered. "It's just that – that those parsley seeds I've planted've come up!"

It sounded lame, even to Lizzie. She babbled on, embroidering. "You see, it's ever so hard to grow parsley seeds, and Mam's tried ever so many times, and then *I* tried, and mine've come up! When they're a bit bigger I shall show her and she'll be ever so pleased. She says a garden's no use without parsley, she says if she had to choose between parsley and mint, she'd pick parsley, any day!"

The longer she went, the worse it sounded.

"But at least it's *true*," she told herself. "That ain't a fib, about the parsley. The only fib is that I didn't really come to tell her that."

The witch herself evidently thought the news not worth the telling. She sat immovable, hugging her knees, not looking, supremely uninterested in parsley, dead or alive.

"I – I expect *you* can grow parsley whenever you want," said Lizzie encouragingly. "I expect you can just spell it to grow."

The witch did not reply. She evidently did not wish even to discuss parsley. Then she vanished.

"Oh!" gasped Lizzie, shocked. Before, the witch had always vanished in a half predictable sort of way, rather triumphantly scoring a point over Lizzie. Today was different. It was as if she had vanished, not of her own accord, but had simply been snuffed out like a candle.

Lizzie stared into the greenish shadow by the hedge, but knew in her bones that the witch would not reappear. For once, she did not even wish her to.

"Goodbye then, witch!" The words drifted forlornly through the unlistening graveyard.

Lizzie turned and trudged back the way she had come, wishing with all her heart that she had not tried to share her news with the witch.

But, once she was down the bank and on the road, her spirits suddenly lifted again. "Yippee! London!" she cried, and ran home.

The Arbuckles were up at six o'clock the next day. Toby and Towser had to be fed, then delivered to Aunt Blodwen.

"Poor little splodge!" said Lizzie, hugging Toby goodbye. "Never mind, Lizzie'll bring you something from London. Hey – what if I see the Queen?"

Toby gurgled and tugged one of her plaits. His eyes were clear and hopeful – he had no idea what was in store for him. (Aunt Blod liked Toby even less than she liked Lizzie.) Now, Lizzie felt half guilty and half wished he were going, after all.

By seven o'clock, the Arbuckles were driving through the quiet, early morning lanes. The low sun lit the hedges to a pale, brilliant green. Every now and then a rabbit darted across their path.

"None of *them* in London," observed Patty. "Except hanging on a hook."

Lizzie winced.

Then they were at the station, then, half an hour later, on the train. Lizzie had only ever been on a train a few times, and then only on a little slow local line, to visit relatives. This was a real train, a fast one, as long as the platform itself, and with kitchens and a buffet car.

"We'll have one of them hot bacon rolls on the way back," said Patty. "We've already had our breakfasts, and the price of things you wouldn't believe."

"Ay, well, we're not to mind a few pence today," said Albert. "Treat, remember."

"Pounds, never mind pence," said Patty.

Lizzie, looking across the table at her father, thought how odd and unfamiliar he looked in his best suit – his only suit, with a collar and tie. What really made him different, though, was the absence of his flat cap, which he wore at home every day of the week. This morning he had automatically taken it from its nail as he went out.

"Not that, Albert," Patty had said warningly. "We don't want folk in London taking us for country bumpkins."

She herself was wearing her best coat, and had a new handbag, which she placed on the table and looked at admiringly from time to time. Lizzie, too, was dressed

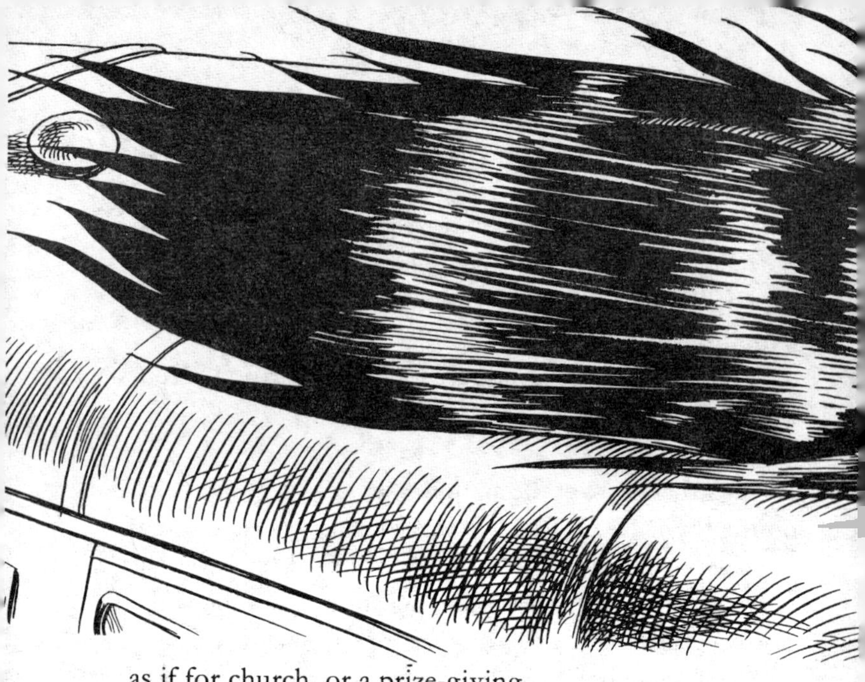

as if for church, or a prize-giving.

"No jeans, Lizzie," Patty had told her. "Not in London."

Lizzie had brought a book of puzzles, but spent the whole journey looking out of the window. Trees, hedges, sheep, churches and houses went racing by, fleet and sunlit. Lizzie was enchanted. She had never been so fast in her life.

"Wonder if this is how it feels to be the witch on her broomstick?" she thought. "Even faster, she might go!"

She wondered where the witch was now, and what she was doing. She even wondered, nervously, whether the witch knew what she, Lizzie, was doing.

"Certainly seems to be able to see things without looking," she thought. "Oooh – wish I hadn't told her that fib!"

But the very idea of the witch crouching on the roof of the train, or flying invisibly level with it, was unim-

aginable, and Albert suggested a game of I Spy, and Lizzie had soon shaken off that dark, threatening presence.

"Don't see how you can play I Spy when things are flying past as soon as you've spied 'em," observed Patty after a while. "Where's that list of yours, Lizzie?"

Albert had suggested that Lizzie make a list of all the things she most wanted to see in London. She fished it out.

"Buckingham Palace, the Queen (if possible), the Changing of the Guard, the Tower of London, Trafalgar Square and the pigeons, Peter Pan's statue, London Zoo and Madame Tussauds."

"Here for the day, not the week, Lizzie," Patty told her.

"Which should you like best?" Albert asked. "Pick two or three."

So Lizzie picked Buckingham Palace, the Tower of London and Madam Tussauds.

"Specially the Chamber of Horrors," she said. "Horrible, that is. Becky Farmer's been. And she says things moved, even if they are wax. Breathed, she said."

"Aye, well, Becky Farmer would," said Patty.

From the moment the Arbuckles reached King's Cross, Lizzie felt in another world. She had never imagined anything so huge, so busy, so noisy. She was dazed. In Little Hemlock, everyone knew everyone else – even if only their names.

"You'd never learn all this lot's names," she thought. "Not in a million years."

Patty had a guide book and was in charge.

"Buckingham Palace first," she said. "Underground."

Down they went on a long silver staircase, moving. At the bottom were long tunnels and warm blowing winds and the roar of trains. And people, hundreds of them, all hurrying – and many of them, Lizzie noticed, wearing jeans. The trains had jaws that opened and shut automatically and spewed people out and swallowed them in. Lizzie felt rather as she did when she'd gone on a fairground ride and then wished, too late, that she hadn't. The main difference being that now she couldn't very well shut her eyes and scream.

Buckingham Palace looked exactly as it did on television and was rather plain for a palace, Lizzie thought. Its only glamour lay in the real toy soldier in his sentry box, and in the flag flying over the roof.

"Means the Queen's in there," Patty told her. "Just imagine!"

Lizzie did try to imagine the Queen in there, and what she was doing. Probably sorting her jewels, she thought, and giving commands.

The Tower of London was not at all a disappointment, in fact, was bigger and better than Lizzie had imagined. She had not known that there were houses in there, that it was a kind of village – though not in the least like Little Hemlock. It was all towering walls, ringing stones.

"Could imagine the witch here," thought Lizzie.

"Caaaaw!" She heard a coarse cry, saw from the corner of her eyes a black raggedy something. Her heart stopped.

"Look, Lizzie," she heard Albert say. "Ravens. Famous they are."

And she did look, and sure enough it *was* ravens, huge, black and glossy, with hard tread and wicked eye.

"Real witches' birds," thought Lizzie. "That's what she'd have for a pet – a raven."

"There always have to be ravens at the Tower," Patty said, consulting the guide book. "Else a curse will fall."

"A curse is another word for a bad spell," thought Lizzie, and said, "Can we see the Crown Jewels now?"

That witch had to be pushed right away. She must

have not even a toehold on Lizzie's special day.

The Crown Jewels were splendid, though it seemed a shame for them to be locked away, hardly ever used.

"If I was queen, I'd dress up every day," Lizzie thought. "I'd wear a crown, anyway. What's the point of being queen if you don't wear a crown?"

Then, inexorably, as if that witch lay in wait for her every thought, "Same as that witch. What if she didn't wear her pointy hat?"

She actually closed her eyes and tried to see her witch dressed like anyone else – Patty, for instance. Lizzie, who could imagine most things, simply could not imagine that witch in skirt and blouse, and certainly not in the hat Patty wore for church. She tried and tried, but the picture simply would not come.

She felt her arm being shaken.

"Here, Lizzie Dripping, *eyes* shut?" said Patty. "We've paid money to see this lot."

"I was just resting them a minute," said Lizzie.

"Dazzled," said Albert. "Isn't it, Lizzie?"

She agreed gratefully.

After the Tower and the Crown Jewels, they found a seat and ate their sandwiches.

"We don't know where the cafes are in London," Patty had said, "*nor* if they give good servings."

Then it was time for Madam Tussauds, the real highlight of the day. Lizzie was deliciously prepared to be appalled and frightened. When Patty saw the queue waiting outside, she was disgusted.

"Have we to stand in that?" she demanded.

Queues never formed in Little Hemlock.

"It's moving ever so fast," said Lizzie quickly. "We shan't have to wait long."

Within half an hour they were inside in another, unreal world of wax figures and sightless eyes – uncanny, unnerving. Patty, in particular, despite her earlier reservations, was enchanted.

"Just look – look!" she kept saying. "Oooh – it's him to the life!"

She simply could not get over it.

"Oooh – it's true, she *is* breathing!" The Sleeping Beauty in her great four-poster bed, breathed and dreamed away her hundred years.

As they entered the Chamber of Horrors the Arbuckles

fell silent. Lizzie looked fearfully about her, and wherever she looked was met by the cold stares of dead eyes. Dead, but seeming to lock your gaze, looking right through you like – like the witch!

And then she saw the witch, dark and dusty in the shadows, eyes glittering. No waxwork this, but a real witch, living and breathing – surely people must notice! The witch grinned.

Lizzie groaned.

"Go away!" She mouthed the words silently. But instead the witch lifted and wagged a warning finger. Lizzie glanced quickly up at her parents, but their eyes were elsewhere. When she looked back, the witch had vanished.

"Did I imagine it?" Anything seemed possible in this weird half world.

Two minutes later the witch was there again, closer this time, her face waxy white, her finger stabbing. Lizzie stared helplessly back at her, riveted by those accusing eyes. She had told a fib, or a sort of fib, and the witch had found her out. Now she was taking her revenge. If she came much closer, Patty and Albert would have to see, have to see that this was no waxwork witch, but a real, living, breathing, spelling witch.

She tugged at Patty's sleeve.

"I don't like it!" she whispered. "I'm scared!"

And she was. Scared that the dungeons in the Chamber of Horrors might soon have three live toads hopping in the shadows, or even – she quaked at the thought – three new figures made out of wax!

"Scared, Lizzie Dripping?" said Patty. "And you spending half your life in a graveyard!"

"Oh, don't!"

She fled then. She fled from the dead eyes of the wax murderers, from the glittering eyes of a real witch, and from what had been, after all, only a very little fib.

Lizzie Dripping and the Two Worlds

The world, it seemed to Lizzie Dripping, was made up of two kinds of things – things that could be counted upon, and things that could not. For instance, you could count upon it that day was followed by night, and vice versa, that eggs hatched into chickens rather than dragons, and that it was always cold meat on Mondays. Lizzie had once started making a list of things you could count on, but had given up at number seventy-nine out of sheer boredom.

Things that could *not* be counted upon were, of course, trickier. You could not be sure of a fine day for a picnic, for instance, or what sort of mood Patty would wake up in, or whether you would get ten out of ten for spelling. You could not count on jigsaws having all their pieces, or Towser sitting up when you told him to, or even on there being a motto in your Christmas cracker.

"But what you really can't count on," Lizzie thought, "is that witch."

She was thinking these thoughts as she cycled slowly through the sun flecked lanes down to the Pingle. In her saddlebag she had a book about wizards, which she meant to spend all morning reading, undisturbed. She was seeing how slowly she could cycle without actually falling off, and at the same time, thinking about the world.

"It would be boring if you could count on everything, the whole time," she thought. "There wouldn't be any surprises. And that witch – she's certainly a surprise, even to me. And what *Mam* would say if she knew . . . ."

What would Patty say if she knew that only last week a witch had followed them all the way from Little Hemlock to London? Lizzie herself could hardly believe it, though she'd seen that witch, all right, in the Chamber of Horrors at Madame Tussauds, pale as wax and eyes a-glitter.

At the very memory, Lizzie wobbled and nearly fell off.

"What if she'd turned *us* to wax, Mam, Dad and me?"

At the time, the possibility had seemed all too likely. Lizzie had run for her life – and knew that she would never hear the end of it. Already half the village knew. Lizzie had not seen the witch since. She'd been to the graveyard once or twice and called, but only half-heartedly. The truth was, she was not altogether sure she could face the witch, having told her a fib.

"Though it wasn't exactly a *proper* fib," she told herself. "More like sort of half a fib, or even a quarter. Shan't think about her, anyway. Think of something else . . . now, where was I . . . ? You can't count on there being any biscuits when you look in the tin – not chocolate ones, anyhow, you can't count on there – whoops!"

She wobbled, then put both feet to the ground, peering downward.

"You can't count on your blessed bike not getting a puncture just when you're off for a nice read! Drat!"

The front tyre was flat as a pancake. Lizzie gave it a kick.

"Trust you!" she told it. "Wait till I'm nearly furthest from home to do it! Spiteful thing! If you don't look out I shall ask for a new bike, for Christmas!"

She glared at the tyre, half hoping that this threat would make it blow up again out of sheer fright, plump as ever.

"Wish *I* was a witch," she said. "I'd spell you up again."

There again, if she were a witch, she would not be wandering about Little Hemlock on a bicycle. For one thing, her cloak might catch in the spokes.

"I'd be on a broomstick," she thought. "And broomsticks don't get flat tyres. P'raps the twigs fall out, though!"

She giggled at the thought. And as she did so, there was a faint but unmistakable whoosh! overhead, and Lizzie Dripping looked up to see a witch sail over on a broomstick.

"My witch!"

Over the waving tops of the high hawthorn hedges, outlined against the blue sky, impossible as snow in August – a witch!

Lizzie dropped her bike onto the bank and waved furiously.

"Witch! Witch – it's me!"

On and up soared the unlikely broomstick with its unlikely passenger, and there floated down a thin, high cackle.

"Witch!" screamed Lizzie.

She had quite forgotten that she dared not face that witch, was scared of her as never before. All she knew was that there, in broad daylight, a witch was riding by on a broomstick. Lizzie always ran, whenever she saw a rainbow, longing to find its end in a hedgerow or a ploughed brown field. With or without a pot of gold it would be the most magical thing. So now she ran to follow that broomstick, to see where it would come down.

"Anywhere," she thought, as she clambered over the stile into the Ten Acre. "Anywhere in the world – world's end, even!"

Lizzie Dripping would normally have thought twice about the desirability of finding herself at the world's end. It might be a lonely – even a frightening place. But when a witch on a broomstick sails past out of the blue, you don't stop to think. You follow.

"Never seen her on a broomstick afore!" she thought. "Must mean something!"

She had played hide-and-seek before with the witch, but never like this. It was not exactly hide-and-seek – more like tag.

"Except I *can't* tag her, not up there!"

The witch was triumphantly up in the air, she herself earthbound. And because Lizzie dared not take her eyes off the witch, she kept running through nettles, screaming, "Owch – oooch!" and then she ran smack into the wooden fence of the Ten Acre.

Over she scrambled and into the wide cow pastures. She hardly saw the cows, though they saw her, lifting their heads and gazing mildly as she flew among them. The witch seemed to be teasing now, treading the air, hovering like a hawk or kestrel. Lizzie came so close that she could see the criss-crossed face, the snapping eyes.

Whoosh! The witch was off again, robes streaming behind her.

"Witch!" screamed Lizzie, with what breath she had, and the scream melted and wasted over the wide turf. The witch was bobbing and ducking now, as if riding invisible waves, and her laughter drifted down to Lizzie in snatches.

Lizzie Dripping kept on, as she had kept on so many times before in pursuit of rainbows. Rainbows might dissolve at any moment and so, as Lizzie well knew, might witches. She reached the far side of the cow pastures and was over the fence and running down the green lane that ended, half a mile away, in the Duke's Wood.

It was beginning to feel to Lizzie as if she were already *at* the world's end. Her legs were heavy and her chest was tight. And the witch was now gaining ground – sky – and was dwindling into the distance until, at a certain moment, she seemed to merge and dissolve into the darkness of the Duke's Wood.

"Oh no!"

Lizzie halted. Gone. Elusive as any rainbow, the witch had

vanished, broomstick and all.

"Mean thing. Mean old thing!" Her eyes stung with disappointment, and strain as she might, there was no sign of anything but the slow, familiar rise of the hedges ahead and the dark shape of the wood. She heard only her own breathing and the curling cries of the lapwings who haunted the place in shoals.

"Gone!"

She knew it, and knew, too, that the witch would not reappear. She had gone riding into her own separate and invisible world, leaving Lizzie high and dry in a world gone suddenly flat and empty.

"Her way of paying me back, I suppose."

She turned and started to retrace her steps, slowly now, and wondering about that sudden visit of the witch, broomstick and all, outside the usual confines of the graveyard.

"Done it to show me she's everywhere, I expect," Lizzie thought. "And if it was to pay me out for that tiny little fib – well, I knew she would, sooner or later. So at least that's over and done with!"

But it wasn't. When Lizzie at last climbed back over the stile from the Ten Acre to the lane where she had left her bike. . . .

"Gone!" She gasped the word, horrorstruck. Horrified, because she knew what Patty would have to say about *that*, and because she felt certain that the bike had not disappeared in an ordinary, everyday kind of way.

"She's had it! Spiteful thing!"

She was paid back now, good and proper.

"Can't go home without it! Daren't!"

The morning was spoilt. The day was spoilt. It seemed to Lizzie that her whole life was spoilt.

"Mum'll say it was my fault, and it wasn't, it wasn't! She don't know about that witch!"

It did not occur to Lizzie Dripping for a single moment that perhaps the witch had not made her bicycle disappear. So certain of it was she, that she began groping among the warm grasses of the bank, in the hope that she might find it there, if only invisibly. And being Lizzie Dripping, she actually imagined what it might be like to have an invisible bike.

"I could wheel it home and mend the puncture and then ride round on an invisible bike! Just pedalling away in thin air! Wouldn't they all boggle!"

She actually laughed at the picture, and it was just her luck that, at that moment, Jake Staples went by.

"Lost summat, Lizzie Dripping? Looking for moles? Looking for daisies, dandies, worms – ?"

"You shut up!" She hissed the words at him. After Aunt Blodwen, Jake Staples was her least favourite person in the whole world.

"You're mad, Lizzie Dripping. Barmy."

As she glared at him, she noticed, sticking from the pocket of his jeans, a catapult. She did not hesitate. She moved swiftly forward and snatched it.

"And *you*, Jake Staples, are a murderer!"

And then she ran.

"Here, you give that back! You – "

On she ran. She seemed to have spent the whole day running. First as pursuer, then as pursued. And now she knew which was worse. When she was chasing the witch, she could have stopped at any minute if she'd wanted, just given up. Now, she had to keep running. If she stopped, Jake Staples would grab the catapult back and go out murdering birds – and as likely as not, give herself a good thumping into the bargain.

Lizzie was a good runner. She won the girls' races at the village sports nearly every year. But Jake was a boy, and bigger than her, and he had not already run himself to a standstill in pursuit of a witch.

"You wait! Just wait till I get you!"

His voice was furious – and close. Lizzie lengthened her stride, ran all out. She ran between the green hedges and back into Little Hemlock and Jake was hard on her heels. She almost thought she could feel his hot breath on her neck. And all the time her mind was working furiously.

"Never make it back home before he catches me! Daren't go back home, anyhow, not without the bike. Oh, what'll I do? Oh, I wish that witch was here!"

She stumbled and half fell, took a quick look over her shoulder and let out a shriek. He was right behind her. She was in Side Lane now, and level with Aunt Blod's neat little cottage. And hardly knowing how the inspiration came, she ran through the open gate, up the path, and pushed the catapult through Aunt Blodwen's letter box!

She turned then, gasping, to face her pursuer. He had stopped short at the gate. None of the children in Little Hemlock ever went to Aunt Blodwen's house – not even on Trick or Treat night, not even at Christmas. For them, who did not have a private witch of their own, Aunt Blodwen was as good as a witch. Even big, bad, bullying Jake Staples dared not set foot in her prim little garden. There was, in any case, no point. That catapult was lying now on the mat beneath Aunt Blodwen's letter box, as safe from Jake as if Lizzie had tossed it into a blazing fire. She knew it, he knew it.

Lizzie did not know whether Aunt Blodwen was in or not. If she were, the door behind her would fly open and

a high Welsh voice would cry: "What's this, what's *this*? *You* Lizzie Dripping, as I might've known!"

But the door did not fly open. Lizzie stayed where she was, recovering her breath. Her eye fell on the wooden bird table with its hanging sacks of nuts and coconut shell. Practically the only good thing about Aunt Blodwen was that she liked birds.

"Better than pets, see," she told Patty. "No mess in the house to be forever cleaning up. Hygienic, birds are. No mess and no clutter. Know where you are, with birds."

"You stopping there all day?" Jake Staples bunched his fist.

"I might," said Lizzie. "Murderer!"

Jake folded his arms.

"You'll have to come out in the end. You wait!"

"And *you* wait!" Lizzie told him. "Aunt Blod likes birds. She's an orner – ornertholer – anyway, she likes 'em. See that bird table?"

His eyes moved to it, and became uneasy.

"Round to your mother like a shot, when she sees that catapult," Lizzie continued. "Does your ma *let* you go round murdering innocent birds?"

She saw him lick his lips. Mrs Staples had five children and no husband. If any of her offspring stepped out of line she thumped them, good and hard. Mrs Staples was the biggest thumper in Little Hemlock. Lizzie knew it, Jake knew it.

"Your Aunt Blod ain't in," said Jake. "She won't know whose catapult it is."

"Not unless I tell her," said Lizzie sweetly. "Don't believe in telling tales, not really. But when it comes to murdering poor, innocent little birds – and think, they might've been the ones that come and peck her nuts. Ever so fond of them, she is. Calls 'em her little pets."

Jake Staples was definitely looking cornered. He was now in danger of getting into more trouble at home than even Lizzie herself, with her lost bike. He licked his lips again.

"I'll do a deal," he said.

"What?"

She expected him to say that he'd let her off a thumping if she promised not to tell Aunt Blodwen who the catapult belonged to.

"Don't tell," he said, "and I'll give your bike back."

Lizzie stared, gobstruck.

"I only meant it as a joke," he said. "Just put it behind the hedge to give you a fright."

He had done that, all right, Lizzie thought. She had been sure that the witch had spirited it away for good, that she'd never set eyes on it again. A long, sweet tide of happiness washed over her.

"Now keep calm, Lizzie," she told herself. "Don't go letting on."

She forced her face into a stern, schoolteacherish look.

"You'll give my bike back, all right, Jake Staples," she told him. "You'll do it this minute. And you'll do something else, as well."

"What?" he demanded, and Lizzie guessed by his voice that he was quaking in his boots now. She had him!

"It's got a puncture," she told him. "You mend it, then fetch it here to me."

"Not here," he begged. "She could be back any minute."

Lizzie recognised the truth of this. She had no more wish to encounter Aunt Blodwen than he had. Innocent as she was, she was bound to be put somehow in the wrong.

"Not here, then," she agreed.

She thought fast.

"Not at home, either. Else Mam might see, and start asking questions. Need never know I lost it, now."

"Where, then?"

"When you've mended the puncture," she said, "leave it in the church porch."

"Right!"

He didn't even stop to ask why. He didn't even jeer: "What – off to the graveyard again, Lizzie Dripping, to see that witch?"

Once, long ago, Lizzie Dripping had unwisely told him that she had seen a witch in the graveyard. He had never forgotten it. His sort wouldn't.

He went straight off, meek as a lamb, to fetch the bike. Lizzie let out a long breath, hardly able to believe her luck. The whole morning, that had seemed shattered, was coming together again. And Lizzie was filled with remorse now, that she had even suspected her witch of so mean a trick.

She went out of the garden, down the road to the church and into the graveyard. And, as she went, she thought again of the way the world was divided into things you could count upon and things you couldn't. When she had set out that morning on her bike, she had meant to spend long, dreamy hours in the Pingle, reading. She could never have guessed that first she would see her witch fly past on a broomstick, and then her bike would disappear, and then she would grab a catapult and post it through Aunt Blodwen's letter box. Never in a million years.

Lizzie turned into the church drive and climbed the steep little pathway to the sky and little knew that the world was about to prove even more unexpected than she had supposed. Her reason for coming to the graveyard at all was not very clear.

"Can hardly expect the witch to be here," she thought. She had, after all, seen that witch not half an hour ago, fizzing past on her broomstick and vanishing into the Duke's Wood. It was a pity, because what Lizzie really wanted was to say sorry to the witch. Sorry, not only for

telling her that teeny, quarter fib, but also for suspecting her of spiriting away Lizzie's bike.

Lizzie was passing the west porch of the church when she heard that familiar, jerky refrain.

"Knit one, slip one, knit one, pass the slip stitch over ... knit one ...."

Lizzie paused for an instant, incredulous, then, "Witch!" she shrieked, and ran round the corner to the church to see that hunched black figure, plain as day and in the real world, there on its accustomed tombstone. Wherever she had been, the witch was back, knitting her way into Lizzie's time and space.

"Oh witch!" said Lizzie, and for a moment felt that she could actually have hugged her, knitting and all. Because a catapult was lying on Aunt Blodwen's mat, a puncture being mended, and the witch – was *smiling* at her! And that, for Lizzie, was the least counted upon thing of all.

Lizzie Dripping in the Snow

Lizzie Dripping had heard the weather forecast last night, and the minute she woke up she remembered it.

"Snow!"

She was up and at the window, pulling back the curtain and meeting the cold air behind it. Out there it was still dark, but she saw at once, by the light of the lamp in the lane, that the promised snow had not come. If it had, she would have been up and dressed in a flash and out there, even in the dark. As it was, she shivered, dropped the curtain and climbed back into the warm, tumbled bed.

"*Never* snows at weekends," she thought.

It was as if the weather had its own calendar, with weekends marked in red, to remind it never to hail, freeze or snow. Albert had promised last night to fetch her old sledge out of the shed and give it a clean down, ready. She could hear him now, down below, raking out the grate, then opening the back door to fetch coal and logs. She lay, half dozing, listening to the familiar pattern of early morning noises – the kettle being filled, pots rattling, then Albert's slow tread up the stairs with Patty's tea. Soon Toby would set up cooing, rattling the bars of his cot – even outright bawling.

When Lizzie awoke for the second time, Patty was there drawing back the curtains.

"What time is it?" Lizzie asked. "It's still dark."

"It's near half past eight," Patty told her, "and dark all day, I shouldn't wonder."

"Why? Why's it dark?"

"You look at that," said Patty. "Snow sky, if ever I saw one."

"Snow!" Lizzie shot up, wide awake in an instant.

Ten minutes later she was dressed and breakfasted and stepping foot into the morning. The minute she did so, she sensed the difference from other, ordinary mornings. For one thing, it was still half dark. The yellowy light from the kitchen spilled onto the stone path. And it was not ordinary, night-time darkness, but a kind of queer half light, a flat greyness. Lizzie looked up and it was as if a ceiling had come down over the world. The sky was dense, heavy.

"A snow sky!" said Lizzie softly, and was certain now that it was only a matter of waiting. And because she wanted to be there at the actual moment when the first few flakes drifted down, she began to walk down the path and stone steps and into the lane.

The sheep in the Home Field moved slowly under the bare trees, where still a few rosy apples hung like lanterns.

"Snow's coming!" Lizzie called to them, and was filled with such unbearable excitement that when it did come, hardly seconds later, it was as if she had *willed* it to come.

First a few tiny specks came twirling down. Then the whole wide sky seemed to ease and relax, and the snow came crowding, flocking out of it in huge, papery flakes. In the twinkling of an eye, the world was altered – it went invisible, almost. All she could see was snow.

"Oh magic!"

And in that instant Lizzie knew where she would go.

"Can't take the sledge out yet, anyhow," she thought. "Have to wait till there's an inch or two."

So she turned on her heel and went back, past her house with its lighted window, over the road and straight to the churchyard. As she pushed open the little iron gate Lizzie paused.

Already the graveyard was being stolen by snow. The stones were capped with it, the grasses whitened. There was a huge, enveloping silence. Even the birds were hushed and invisible.

"And I'm invisible, as well," thought Lizzie. "No one can see *me*."

It was a strange thought. She had often thought what a wonderful thing it would be to go invisible, and this was perhaps the closest she would ever come to it.

"Makes you feel almost as if – as if you're not *real*," she thought, and was glad of the cold touch of the flakes on her face, to reassure her that she was.

"Fish fingers!" she said firmly, out loud. It was a kind of charm, to remind her of that other world, the one everybody called real. Lizzie was not so sure. When she was in the graveyard with the witch it felt real enough to her. Too real, sometimes.

As she hesitated, Lizzie pictured the witch cross-legged on her slab and wreathed in snow, the brim and tip of her steepling hat already white. That decided it. That was a picture she had to see with her own eyes.

And so she did. She passed the corner of the church and her eyes went straight to the tomb of *Hannah Post of this parish and Albert Cyril, beloved husband of the above 1802–1879 Peace, Perfect Peace.* There, by the hedge, was a blurred black shape that could only be the witch.

"Oh witch!" Lizzie ran to greet her.

There was no knitting today, and no book. The witch was sitting in a hunch like a badly wrapped parcel, her mitted fingers lost somewhere in her voluminous robes. Lizzie stopped, as usual, a few feet away. She had never gone *really* close to the witch, and certainly had never touched her. Now, through the dividing curtain of snow she saw, incredibly, something else. Did the witch *know* that she had a robin perched on her hat?

"Shows how magical she is," Lizzie thought. "You'd never get a robin perching on an ordinary person's hat, never!"

The person who wore hats most was Aunt Blod, and Lizzie certainly couldn't see a robin sitting on *her* head.

She stood and looked, and they looked back, the witch and the robin both. Lizzie had a sudden thought, and being Lizzie, said it straight out loud.

"Witch," she said, "do you have a cat?"

Most witches did. But then this was a particularly

offbeat witch, who would be quite capable of having a robin instead of a cat.

"Cat?" repeated the witch.

"Yes – have you got one? A black one?"

"Can't abide 'em," said the witch. "Nasty spitting things. If *I* see cats, I turn 'em into toads!"

This was true. The very first spell Lizzie had seen the witch do was turn the Briggs's cat into a toad. It had frightened the living daylights out of her, at the time. And even now, it seemed a good idea to steer the conversation away from the subject of toads.

"Better not tell her about the bird," she thought, "else she might turn *that* toad."

She tried hard not even to look at the robin on the witch's hat.

"Isn't it smashing?" she offered.

The witch did not reply.

"All this!" She waved her arms to indicate the whirling flakes.

"Nasty wet stuff!" snapped the witch unhelpfully. "I can do without snow in my bones, and I can do without *you*!"

Lizzie didn't much like the sound of this. It sounded like a threat to make Lizzie herself disappear, rather.

"I shan't stop long," she promised. "I just – just wanted to *see* you in the snow. It suits you, it does really. Black and white together – it looks smashing. You know – a really good match!"

The witch gazed back at her, unmoved by this compliment.

"I'm going sledging in a bit," Lizzie told her. "On Parson Hill. It's ever so steep, and you have to watch out you don't run into the trees."

"Sledging?" repeated the witch. "What's sledging?"

"It – it's sort of getting on this wooden thing, with sort of runners, and whizzing down hills!"

The definition sounded unsatisfactory, even to herself. And clearly the witch could make neither head nor tail of it. Lizzie had a sudden inspiration.

"You come!" she cried. "You can come on my sledge with me – there's room for two."

It was marvellous, irresistible, the idea of rushing helter-skelter down Parson Hill, with a real live witch!

"It'd be sort of like being on a broomstick, except in the snow instead of the air!"

The witch was nodding.

"I'll come!" she announced – and vanished. It happened so suddenly that Lizzie did not exactly see it, but she could have sworn that, in that instant, she glimpsed something small and brown flutter off into the mazy snow.

"Robin didn't vanish, then," she thought. "So it wasn't hers, instead of a cat."

As Lizzie trudged out of Little Hemlock, pulling her sledge, she was beginning to have second thoughts about her invitation to the witch.

"She'll have to put her arms round me, to hang on," she thought. "Don't know if I'd like that. And what if I run into one of them trees and it tips her off? Won't like that. 'Do without snow,' she said."

There was certainly plenty of snow now for the witch to do without – a good six inches, and still coming. The world was empty, hushed. There were no cars, and if there were any people about they were hidden and their

footsteps muffled. Lizzie stopped and listened. There was a huge, unearthly silence. The flakes swarmed like great white bees, and staring into them made her dizzy.

"You could disappear in this," she thought. "Disappear and never be seen again."

She looked behind her and saw that already her footprints were filling. Soon there would be no trace of them.

"That witch ..." she thought. "Wonder if *she* leaves footprints ...?"

And immediately she was excited by the thought that soon she would find out – one of her questions would be answered.

"If she does, then she must be real. Really real." Then, as an afterthought, "And even if she don't, it doesn't mean to say she's not real in a way ...."

Lizzie Dripping liked to have her cake and eat it too.

She was trying to find the gate that led onto Parson Hill when the world was suddenly peopled again. She heard voices, screams and yells, and one voice she could hear above all the rest. It was that of Mr Craven, the scoutmaster.

"Old bossyboots," she muttered. "Trying to organise everbody, I expect."

By the time she found the gate she met everyone else coming out of it.

"Come along – all of you. Come on – out!" It was Mr Craven, pulling a sledge.

"What's happening?" Lizzie was bewildered.

"Spoil sport!" she heard, and "Trust him!"

"Davy Cartwright's hit his head, that's what's happened," said Mr Craven. "Smack into a tree."

"He's not *dead*!" came another voice – Jake Staples'.

"Could've been, though. Come on, Lizzie, with us.

There's to be no more sledging till the snow's stopped. Too dangerous."

Lizzie could see Davy Cartwright on the sledge, clutching his head and whimpering.

"Look sharp now, Lizzie," said Mr Craven. "Can't see your hand in front of your face in this lot. Don't want any more accidents."

"But . . . but I arranged to meet someone here," Lizzie stammered. "She'll be wondering where I am."

"Nobody left out there," Mr Craven told her. He cupped his hands and bawled.

"Over here! Over here! Anyone still out there?"

Lizzie held her breath. Surely, surely that witch would not emerge blackly through those crowding flakes?

"Any case, she's got no wellies," she told herself. She crossed her fingers just the same.

"Probably meet her on the way back," Mr Craven told her.

Lizzie fervently hoped not, and kept her fingers crossed (though this was not an easy matter in damp woolly gloves). She trudged gloomily back towards the village, tailing behind the rest.

"That witch *said* she'd come," she thought. "What if she does, and I'm not there?"

It was a serious matter to break a promise to anyone. But to break a promise to a witch!

"Could do anything, when she finds out. Any case, wanted to go sledging, I did."

The snow was falling in a thick curtain, and curtains are very useful in a game of hide-and-seek. All Lizzie had to do was stand still, and watch the shapes of the rest dissolving away into the whiteness, and hear their voices fade. The huge snow silence returned.

"I ain't scared," said Lizzie Dripping. But she was, ever so slightly. She was scared at the idea of being alone with the witch on Parson Hill. She hesitated. She had made a promise. She turned and went back the way she had come, out of the lane, out of the village, out of the world, it seemed.

She trudged on for what seemed like ages. The snow and the silence grew denser. A wind blew up, and it blew into Lizzie's face and lifted the fallen snow into a white mist.

"Blowing footprints away!" she thought, and strained to find marks of boots and sledges, and couldn't. "Am I going the wrong way?"

Had she taken the wrong road where it forked outside the village – or worse, was she following one of the green lanes that threaded the fields? She tried not to think of stories she had heard of people going round and round in circles till they dropped with exhaustion. She strained her eyes for sight of a familiar landmark. All she could make out, now and then, was the occasional tree. This was no comfort. One tree is very like another, unless it is a blasted oak, or stands in a row like the great beeches away at the other end of the village. Lizzie Dripping thought she knew Little Hemlock like the back of her own hand. Now she felt like a stranger in a foreign land.

"I ain't frit!" She said it out loud. She plodded on. But now she was beginning to wonder how long she had been walking.

"Drat – no watch!" She had left it off in case the snow got into its works in a tumble from the sledge, or a snowball fight.

Time and space were both dissolving now in this white world. The snowflakes fell incessantly, dancing and spinning. Lizzie was giddy now, and becoming desperate. She had forgotten Parson Hill and the witch. All she wanted was to get home. She tried to picture it, with its light and warm fire, and Toby on the rug with his bricks, and Patty rattling about in the scullery. It was there, still there, anchored in this alien whiteness. She stopped, panting. Nothing. No sight, no sound, only the inexorably falling snow.

"Fish fingers!" she screamed. "Fish fingers!"

And, as it was intended as a charm, so it worked like one. Because, in that instant, she *did* make out a familiar shape, a dark smudge in that white world.

"Oh witch, witch!" And Lizzie Dripping burst into tears.

Afterwards, try as she might, she could never remember exactly what happened. She thought – only thought – that she had actually felt the witch's touch for the very first time, had crept into the comfort of her enfolding robes.

Nor could she remember what the witch had said. All she knew for certain was that one moment she had been lost and frightened, and the next she was sitting on her sledge and being drawn, fast as the wind, over the snow. Ahead, grasping the ropes, went the witch, robes flapping so that she seemed like some giant bird. Lizzie did not

know whether the witch was actually flying, but she was certainly skimming the snow, going in long, sweeping strides like a skater on ice.

It was a strange journey, and silent, but for the soft sough of the wind. The witch went gliding and Lizzie went gliding fast, fast, through the mazy snow. It might have lasted for seconds, it might have been hours. It was as if she were being drawn through a hole in time itself.

Just as Lizzie could never remember the beginning of that journey, nor could she remember the end. She supposed that the witch, her rescue ended, had simply dissolved wordlessly into the snow. She might have been frightened off by the sound of human voices, because voices there were, surprised and anxious.

"Lizzie Dripping! You? Whatever . . . ?"

"Look at you, child, half frozen!"

And then she was indoors, dazed by the sudden light and warmth, and someone was pulling off her sodden things and someone was saying, "I'll give Patty and Albert a ring – let them know she's safe."

Then there was the fire, the mug of soup, the hot-aches in fingers and toes. And later, of course, the tellings off. These were not as bad as they might have been, because nobody knew that Lizzie had been lost and alone, had thought she was walking right off the edge of the world. Nobody knew that, or ever would know, but Lizzie Dripping herself – and, of course, the witch.

also published by BBC Children's Books:

Lizzie Dripping on Holiday

HELEN CRESSWELL

Lizzie Dripping is excited because it's the last day of school, and the whole of the summer holidays lie ahead – long, lazy days all to herself. But the witch who lives in the graveyard just won't leave her in peace. And unfortunately, Lizzie has promied to come and visit her every single day, and "them as breaks promises pay forfeits". After Lizzie neglects her promise, the witch pops up everywhere and threatens to turn people inot crabs, toads and goodness knows what else . . .

These six delightful stories first appeared in two BBC paperbacks, *Lizzie Dripping and the Little Angel* and *Lizzie Dripping by the Sea*.